T5-DGH-229

R00464 01618

CHICAGO PUBLIC LIBRARY
WOODSON REGIONAL

R0046401618

OCT 1985 The
Chicago Public Library

PS
3560
.073
I5

1965

WOODSON REGIONAL
LIBRARY CENTER
9525 SOUTH HALSTED STREET
CHICAGO, ILLINOIS 60628

LIVING
ROOM

Other Books by June Jordan

Who Look at Me • Soulscript • The Voice of the Children

Some Changes • His Own Where • Dry Victories

*Fannie Lou Hamer • New Days: Poems of Exile and Return
• New Life: New Room*

*Passion, 1977–1980 • Civil Wars
• Things that I do in the dark*

Kimako's Story • On Call;

LIVING ROOM

NEW POEMS BY
JUNE JORDAN

THUNDER'S MOUTH PRESS · NEW YORK · CHICAGO

Copyright © 1985 by June Jordan
All rights reserved
Published in the United States by Thunder's Mouth
Press Inc., Box 780, New York N.Y. 10025 and Box
11223 Chicago, Il. 60611
Design by Juanita E. Gordon
Grateful acknowledgement is made to the New
York State Council on the Arts and the National
Endowment for the Arts for financial assistance
with the publication of this volume.

Some of these poems have previously been pub-
lished in *The Literary Review, The Iowa Review,
13th Moon, Feminist Studies, The Little Magazine,
Helicon Nine, Poetry East, Home Girls: An Anthol-
ogy of Black Feminism, The Search: The Journal of
Islamic Studies, Confirmations, Freedomways,
Ikon, The River Styx, Northwest Review, Open
Places, The Village Voice, La Barricada, Casa de
Las Americas, And Not Surrender, Alert, Southern
Exposure, ACM, Emergency, Denver Quarterly,
Essence*

Photo by Sharon Farmer

Library of Congress Cataloging in Publication
Data
Jordan, June, 1936–
   Living room.

I. Title.
PS3560.0′73L5   1985   811′.54   84-24030
ISBN 0-938410-27-X
ISBN 0-938410-26-1 (pbk.)

REF
PS
3560
.073
L5
1985
cp 2

Distributed by
PERSEA BOOKS
225 Lafayette St.
N.Y. N.Y. 10012
212-431-5270

ontents

Poem

Contents Cont'd

dreams
arms
doors
air

ash

dreams
arms
doors
air

dedicated
to the children of Atlanta
and
to the children of Lebanon

1

Natural order is being restored
Natural order means you take a pomegranate
that encapsulated plastic looking orb complete
with its little top/a childproof cap that you can
neither twist nor turn
and you keep the pomegranate stacked inside a wobbly
pyramid composed by 103 additional pomegranates
next to a sign saying 89 cents
each

Natural order is being restored
Natural order does not mean a pomegranate
split open to the seeds sucked by the tongue and lips
while teeth release the succulent sounds
of its voluptuous disintegration

The natural order is not about a good time
This is not a good time to be against
the natural order

(voices from the background)

"Those Black bitches tore it up! Yakkety
yakkety complain complaints couldn't see
no further than they got to have this
they got to have that they got to have
my job, Jack: my job!"

"To me it was Black men laid us wide open for the cut.
Busy telling us to go home. Sit tight.
Be sweet. So busy hanging tail and chasing
tail they didn't have no time to take a good
look at the real deal."

"Those macho bastards! They would rather blow
the whole thing up than give a little: It was
vote for spite: vote white for spite!"

"Fucken feminists turned themselves into bulldagger
dykes and scared the shit out of decent
smalltown people: That's what happened."

"Now I don't even like niggers but there they were
chewing into the middle of my paycheck
and not me but a lot of other white people
just got sick of it, sick of carrying
the niggers."

"Old men run the government: You think that's
their problem?
Everyone of them is old and my parents and the old
people get out big numbers of them, voting for the dead"

"He's eighteen just like all the rest.
Only thing he wants is a girl and a stereo
and hanging out hanging out. What
does he care about the country? What
did he care?"

Pomegranates 89¢ each

2

Frozen cans of orange juice.
Pre-washed spinach.
Onions by the bag.
Fresh pineapple with a printed
message from the import company.
Cherry tomatoes by the box.
Scallions rubberbanded by the bunch.
Frozen cans of orange juice.
Napkins available.
No credit please.

3

This is not such a hot
time for you or for me.

4

Natural order is being restored.
Designer jeans will be replaced by the designer
of the jeans.
Music will be replaced by reproduction
of the music.
Food will be replaced by information.
Above all the flag is being replaced by the flag.

5

This was not a good time to be gay

Shortly before midnight a Wednesday
massacre felled eight homosexual Americans
and killed two: One man was on his way
to a delicatessen and the other
on his way to a drink. Using an Israeli
submachine gun the killer fired into the crowd
later telling police about the serpent in the garden
of his bloody heart, and so forth

This was not a good time to be Black

Yesterday the Senate passed an anti-busing
rider and this morning the next head
of the Senate Judiciary said he would work
to repeal the Voter Registration
Act and this afternoon the Greensboro
jury fully acquitted members of the Klan
and the American Nazi party in the murder
of 5 citizens and in Youngstown Ohio and in
Chattanooga
Tennessee and in Brooklyn and in Miami
and in Salt Lake City and in Portland Oregon
and in Detroit Michigan
and in Los Angeles and in Buffalo
Black American women and men
were murdered and the hearts
of two of the victims were carved
from the bodies of the victims, etcetera

This was not a good time to be old

Streamliner plans for the Federal Budget
include elimination of Social Security
as it exists; and similarly Medicare and Medicaid
face severe reevaluation, among other things.

This was not a good time to be young

Streamliner plans also include elimination
of the Office of Education and the military
draft becomes a drastic concern as the national
leadership boasts that this country will no longer
be bullied and blackmailed by wars for liberation
or wars
for independence elsewhere on the planet, and the like.

*This was not a good time to be a pomegranate ripening
on a tree*

This was not a good time to be a child

Suicide rates among the young reached
alltime highs as the incidence of child
abuse and sexual abuse
rose dramatically across the nation.
In Atlanta Georgia at least twenty-eight Black
children have been murdered, with
several more missing and all of them feared dead, or
something of the sort.

This was not a good time to be without a job

Unemployment Compensation and the minimum
wage have been identified as programs
that plague the poor and the young
who really require different incentives
towards initiative/pluck and so forth

This was not a good time to have a job

Promising to preserve traditional
values of freedom, the new administration
intends to remove safety regulations
that interfere
with productivity potential, etcetera.

This was not a good time to be a woman

Pursuing the theme of traditional values of freedom
the new leadership has pledged its
opposition to the Equal Rights Amendment
that would in the words of the President-elect
only throw the weaker sex into a vulnerable
position among mischievous men, and the like.

This was not a good time to live in Queens

Trucks carrying explosive nuclear wastes will
exit from the Long Island Expressway and then
travel through residential streets of Queens
en route to the 59th Street Bridge, and so on.

This was not a good time to live in Arkansas

Occasional explosions caused by mystery
nuclear missiles have been cited
as cause for local alarm, among
other things.

This was not a good time to live in Grand Forks
North Dakota

Given the presence of a United States nuclear
missile base in Grand Forks North Dakota
the non-military residents of the area feel
that they are living only a day by day distance
from certain
annihilation, etcetera.

This was not a good time to be married.

The Pope has issued directives concerning
lust that make for difficult interaction
between otherwise interested parties

This was not a good time not to be married.
This was not a good time to buy a house
at 18% interest.
This was not a good time to rent housing
on a completely decontrolled
rental market.
This was not a good time to be a Jew
when the national Klan agenda targets
Jews as well as Blacks among its
enemies of the purity of the people
This was not a good time to be a tree
This was not a good time to be a river
This was not a good time to be found with a gun
This was not a good time to be found without one
This was not a good time to be gay
This was not a good time to be Black
This was not a good time to be a pomegranate
or an orange
This was not a good time to be against
the natural order

—Wait a minute—

6

Sucked by the tongue and the lips
while the teeth release the succulence
of all voluptuous disintegration

I am turning under the trees
I am trailing blood into the rivers
I am walking loud along the streets
I am digging my nails and my heels into the land
I am opening my mouth
I am just about to touch the pomegranates
piled up precarious

7

This is a good time
This is the best time
This is the only time to come together

Fractious
Kicking
Spilling
Burly
Whirling
Raucous
Messy

Free

Exploding like the seeds of a natural disorder.

in the february blizzard of 1983
this boy asking me do I know why
this is Black history month I
go sure I know
it's because of the snow

Des Moines Iowa Rap

So his wife and his daughters could qualify
Lester Williams told the people he was gonna try suicide:
suicide.
He promised the papers he would definitely try
so his wife and his babies could qualify for welfare
in the new year.
Welfare.
In the new year.

I wanna job so bad I can taste it I won't waste it
Wanna job so bad

36 years old and home from the Navy
Take my blood, he said, and my bones, he said,
for the meat and the gravy/I'm a vet from the Navy!
Take my meat. Take my bones.
I'm a blood, he said.

Tried suicide. Tried suicide.

Lester Williams made the offer and the offer made news
Wasn't all that much to dispute and confuse
Wouldn't hide in no closet and under no bed
Said he'd straightaway shoot himself dead instead
Like a man
Like a natural man
Like a natural man wanna job so bad he
can taste it
he can taste it

Took the wife in his arms. Held the children in his heart.
Took the gun from his belt. Held the gun to his head.
Like a man.
Like a natural man.
Like a natural man wanna job so bad gotta waste it.
Gotta waste it.

Tried Suicide.
Tried Suicide.

A poem for Jonathan

Land cloven by the water
fall and rush the pushed
down slabs of wetbelly
slate rocks crashing up

This place so steep the trees
brake deep against the edges
of a lifelong avalanche held
more than momentarily by maple
or by cedar roots against this excitable
mountain slide
into lagoon and proliferating
tiny flowers wild
as Jonathan stands gentle
as the stars that follow tall
above it all
saying, "Yes:
This is a wilderness."

So little I could hold the edges
of your earth inside my arms

Your coffee skin the cotton stuff
the rain makes small

Your boundaries of sea and ocean slow
or slow escape possession

Even a pig would move towards you
dignified from mud

Your inside walls a pastel stucco
for indelible graffiti:

movimiento del pueblo
unido

A handkerchief conceals the curling
of your outlaw lips

A pistol calms the trembling
of your fingers

I imagine you among the mountains
eating early rice

I remember you among the birds
that do not swallow blood

rst poem from Nicaragua Libre:
teotecacinte

Can you say Teotecacinte?
Can you say it,
Teotecacinte?

Into the dirt she fell
she blew up the shell
fell into the dirt the artillery
shell blew up the girl
crouching near to the well of the little house
with the cool roof thatched on the slant
the little girl of the little house fell
beside the well unfinished for water
when that mortar
shattered the dirt under her barefeet
and scattered pieces of her four
year old anatomy
into the yard dust and up
among the lower branches of a short tree

Can you say it?

That is two and a half inches of her scalp there
with the soft hairs stiffening
in the grass

Teotecacinte
Can you say it,
Teotecacinte?

Can you say it?

cond poem from Nicaragua Libre:
war zone

On the night road from El Rama the cows
congregate fully in the middle and you
wait
looking at the cowhide colors bleached
by the high stars above their bodies
big with ribs

At some point you just have to trust
somebody else the soldier
wearing a white shirt the poet
wearing glasses the woman
wearing red shoes
into combat

At dawn the student gave me a caramel
candy and pigs and dogs ran into the streets
as the sky began the gradual
wide burn and towards the top
of a new mountain I saw
the teen-age shadows of two sentries
armed with automatics
checking the horizon
for slow stars

from Nicaragua Libre:
photograph of managua

The man is not cute.
The man is not ugly.
The man is teaching himself
to read.
He sits in a kitchen chair
under a banana tree.
He holds the newspaper.
He tracks each word with a finger
and opens his mouth to the sound.
Next to the chair the old V-Z rifle
leans at the ready.
His wife chases a baby pig with a homemade
broom and then she chases her daughter running
behind the baby pig.
His neighbor washes up with water from the barrel
after work.
The dirt floor of his house has been swept.
The dirt around the chair where he sits
has been swept.
He has swept the dirt twice.
The dirt is clean.
The dirt is his dirt.
The man is not cute.
The man is not ugly.
The man is teaching himself
to read.

ourth poem from Nicaragua Libre:
Report from the Frontier

gone gone gone ghost
gone
both the house of the hard dirt floor and the church
next door
torn apart more raggedy than skeletons
when the bombs hit
leaving a patch of her hair on a piece of her scalp
like bird's nest
in the dark yard still lit by flowers

I found
the family trench empty
the pails of rainwater standing full
a soldier whistling while thunder invaded
the afternoon
shards
shreds
one electric bulb split by bullets
dead hanging plants
two Sandinistas riding donkeys
a child sucking a mango
many dogs lost
five seconds left above the speechless
tobacco fields
like a wooden bridge you wouldn't
trust
with the weight of a cat

Safe

The Río Escondido at night
in between
jungle growing down to the muddy
edges of deep water possibilities
       helicopter attack
       alligator assault
       contra confrontations
       blood sliding into the silent scenery
where I sat cold and wet
but surrounded by five
compañeros
in a dugout canoe

rections for Carrying Explosive
Nuclear Wastes through
Metropolitan New York

Enter the Long Island Expressway at Brookhaven.
Proceed West. Exit at Hoyt Street in Astoria.
Turn left onto Astoria Boulevard. Trundle
under the elevated tracks there. Turn
right to ramp for the 59th Street Bridge.
Cross the Bridge. Follow local streets travelling
West until Amsterdam Avenue. At Amsterdam
turn right. Proceed North.

Special Note to Drivers of Trucks Carrying
Explosive Nuclear Wastes through
Metropolitan New York:

Check oil levels every five miles.
Change fan belt every thousand.
Check tire pressure every morning.
Change tires.
Buy radials.
Check shocks every fifty miles.
Change shocks every hundred.
Check rearview mirror and sideview mirror
incessantly.
Keep eyes on road.
Grant all other vehicles and each pedestrian
the right of way.

Do not pass.
Do not drive in the rain.
Do not drive in the snow.
Do not drive in the dark.
Signal.
Use headlights on high beam.
Go slow.
Do not brake suddenly or
otherwise.
Think about your mother
and look out for the crazies.

reensboro: North Carolina:
Dedicated to Constance Evans

We
studying the rule
you can
not say death to the Klan
you can
not say death to the Klan
            death to the Klan
you can
not say death to the Klan

We
answering the riddle
why the white
man will not give the black
man
a glass of water
why the white
man will not give
the black man
a glass of water why
the white
man will not give the black
man death to the Klan
you can
not say a glass of water
to a thirsty black man

you cannot
say
a glass of water
you cannot
say
death to the Klan

death to the Klan

roblems of Translation:
Problems of Language
Dedicated to Myriam Díaz-Diocaretz

1

I turn to my Rand McNally Atlas.
Europe appears right after the Map of the World.
All of Italy can be seen page 9.
Half of Chile page 29.
I take out my ruler.
In global perspective Italy
amounts to less than half an inch.
Chile measures more than an inch and a quarter
of an inch.
Aproximately
Chile is as long as China
is wide:
Back to the Atlas:
Chunk of China page 17.
All of France page 5: As we say in New York:
Who do France and Italy know
at Rand McNally?

2

I see the four mountains in Chile higher
than any mountain of North America.
I see Ojos del Salado the highest.
I see Chile unequivocal as crystal thread.
I see the Atacama Desert dry in Chile more than the rest
of the world is dry.
I see Chile dissolving into water.
I do not see what keeps the blue land of Chile
out of blue water.
I do not see the hand of Pablo Neruda on the blue land.

3

As the plane flies flat to the trees
below Brazil
below Bolivia
below five thousand miles below
my Brooklyn windows
and beside the shifted Pacific waters
welled away from the Atlantic at Cape Horn
La Isla Negra that is not an island La
Isla Negra
that is not black
is stone and stone of Chile
feeding clouds to color
scale and undertake terrestial forms
of everything unspeakable.

4

In your country how
do you say copper
for my country?

5

Blood rising under the Andes and above
the Andes blood
spilling down the rock
corrupted by the amorality
of so much space
that leaves such little trace of blood
rising to the irritated skin the face
of the confession far
from home:

I confess I did not resist interrogation.
I confess that by the next day I was no longer sure
of my identity
I confess I knew the hunger.
I confess I saw the guns.
I confess I was afraid.
I confess I did not die.

6

What you Americans call a boycott
of the junta?
Who will that feed?

7

Not just the message but the sound.

8

Early morning now and I remember
corriente a la madrugada from a different
English poem,
I remember from the difficulties of the talk
an argument
athwart the wine the dinner and the dancing
meant to welcome you
you did not understand the commonplace expression
of my heart:

the truth is in the life
la verdad de la vida

Early morning:
Do you say *la mañanita*?
But then we lose
the idea of the sky uncurling to the light:

Early morning and I do not think we lose:
the rose we left behind
broken to a glass of water on the table
at the restaurant stands
even sweeter
por la mañanita

Independence Day in the U.S.A.

I wanted to tell you about July 4th
in northamerica and the lights computerized
shrapnel in white
or red or fast-fuse blue
to celebrate the only revolution
that was legitimate
in human history

I wanted to tell you about the baby
screaming this afternoon where the park
and the music of thousands who eat
food and stay hungry or homicidal
on the subways or the windowsills of the city
came together loud
like the original cannon shots
from that only legitimate revolution
in human history

I wanted to tell you about my Spanish
how it starts like a word aggravating the beat
of my heart then rushes up to my head
where my eyes dream Carribean
flowers and my mouth waters
around black beans
or coffee that lets me forget
the hours before morning

But I am living inside the outcome
of the only legitimate revolution
in human history
and the operator will not place my call to Cuba
the mailman will not carry my letters to Managua
the State Department will not okay my visa
for a short-wave conversation
and you do not speak English

and I can dig it

I am the fallen/I am the cliff

After the last building the black and green river
pearls into darkness
Beyond the bars on my window the wind bangs every
bridge into the tree tops
Even the city sky becomes unspeakable
as flesh
See the white horse missing from the poem

To Sing a Song of Palestine

for Shula Koenig (Israeli Peace Activist)

All the natural wonders that don't grow there
(Nor tree nor river nor a great plains lifting grain
nor grass nor rooted fruit and
vegetables) forever curse the land
with wildly dreaming schemes
of transformation
military magic
thick accomplishments of blood.

I sing of Israel and Palestine:
The world as neither yours nor mine:
How many different men will fit
themselves how fast
into that place?

A woman's body as the universal
shelter to the demon or the sweet as paradigm
of home that starts and ends with face
to face surrendering to the need
that each of us can feed or take
away
amazing as the space created
by the mothers of our time
—can we behold ourselves
   like that
the ribs the breathing muscles and the fat
of everything desire requires
for its rational abatement?

I write beside the rainy sky
tonight an unexpected an American
cease-fire to the burning day
that worked like war across my
empty throat before I thought to try this way
to say I think we can: I think we can.

1   On the Road

Once in awhile
it's like calling home long distance but nobody
lives there anymore

2   New Hampshire

White mountains or trout
streams or rocks sharp as a fighter plane
simply afloat
above the superhighways

Almost by herself
(trying to "live free or die")
a white girl twitching white tears
unpolluted under the roar
of Pease Air Force Base immortalized
by flyboys taking out Hiroshima
but now
real interested just to take her out
anywhere at all

This is not racist

3 Brooklyn

Running imagery through the arteries of her
pictures posted up against apartheid
what does a young Black poet do?
What does a young
Black woman poet
do
after dark?

Six dollars in her backpack
carrying the streets like a solitary
sentinel possessed by visions
of new arms new
partners

what does she do?

What does the Black man
in his early thirties
in a bomber jacket
what does the Black man do about the poet
when he sees her?

After he took the six
dollars
After he punched her
down
After he pushed for pussy
After he punctured her lungs with his knife
After the Black man
in his early thirties
in a bomber jacket
After she stopped bleeding
After she stopped pleading
(*please don't hurt me*)

what was the imagery running
through the arteries of the heart
of that partner?

This is not racist

3 New Bedford

The lady wanted to have a drink
The lady wanted to have two drinks

Four men dragged the lady to the table
Two men blocked the door
All of them laughing
Four men
Two men
All of them laughing
A lot of the time the lady could not
breathe
A lot of the time the lady wanted
to lose consciousness

Six men
One lady

All of them Portuguese

This is a promise I am making
it here
legs spread on the pool
table of New Bedford

I am not racist

I am raising my knife
to carve out the heart
of no shame

5 On the Road

This is the promise
I am making it here on the road
of my country

I am raising my knife
to carve out the heart
of no shame

The very next move is not mine

July 4, 1984:   For Buck
April 7, 1978–June 16, 1984

You would shrink back/jump up
cock ears/shake head
tonight
at this bloody idea of a birthday
represented by smackajack explosions
of percussive lunacy and downright
(blowawayavillage) boom boom
ratatat-tat-zap

Otherwise any threat would make you stand
quivering perfect as a story
no amount of repetition could hope to ruin
perfect as the kangaroo boogie you concocted
with a towel in your jaws and your tail
tucked under and your paws
speeding around the ecstatic circle
of your refutation of the rain
outdoors

And mostly you would lunge electrical
and verge into the night
ears practically on flat alert
nostrils on the agitated sniff
(for falling rawhide meteors) and laugh
at compliments galore and then
teach me to love you
by hand
teach me to love you
by heart

as I do now

poem for Dana

1

Back in Minneapolis I became convinced
that swimming in the hotel pool with none of the water
over my head and all of the water warm as tea
was maximal security

Back and forth across the lovely public
tub I used my backstroke while I
counted up the blizzard clouds
above the low glass roof
above my nose

Any other city you'd see vast erratic downtown
tracts of wasting space specific as the blowing
garbage or the car parts turned to rust
on stony rubble swelling as now
the shadows slight
those planted trees as delicate as the surrounding
snow
stuck to steel construction cranes that red
and yellow sway
intentional across the frozen ground

2

Into Iowa and I
flying arms folded cold against the view
of trees extremely occasional below on flatland
unresponsive to the everywhere bending sky
I
did not expect you suddenly large suddenly
close beside me in a car or elevator
miles of heat away from outdoor details
like the stalks of pig corn sturdy on the light
blue dirt or rosy hogs loose in late
morning or the rooted quadrupeds the black
clump cattle paralyzed on rounded sightlines icy
as the earth itself

3

who can move from space to flesh
who can knit her own wool cap to wear
who can make the coffee makes the rest of it seem
easier

4

adding the strawberries
adding the cream

5

Willow
Salix (species unknown)
who names the tree poor at the end of the Union
Footbridge bounced under my body absorbing the night
like birch
bark harboring stars in the heavyweight
snowstorm circling
the lips the eyelashes
river making the ice move
under me
the Iowa river making ice move

33,000 feet high and over one wing of the Ozark
DC-9 Fan
Jet I
look for the place to build you a house
only of snow

Song for Soweto

At the throat of Soweto
a devil language falls
slashing
claw syllables to shred and leave
raw
the tongue of the young
girl
learning to sing
her own name

Where she would say
     water
They would teach her to cry
      blood
Where she would save
     grass
They would teach her to crave
       crawling into the
       grave
Where she would praise
     father
They would teach her to pray
      somebody please
      do not take him
     away
Where she would kiss with her mouth
      my homeland
They would teach her to swallow
      this dust

But words live in the spirit of her face and that
sound will no longer yield to imperial erase

Where they would draw
                          blood
She will drink
                    water
Where they would deepen
                            the grave
She will conjure up
                      grass
Where they would take
                        father and family away
She will stand
                  under the sun/she will stay
Where they would teach her to swallow
                                        this dust
She will kiss with her mouth
                              my homeland
and stay
with the song of Soweto

stay
with the song of Soweto

lantic Coast Reggae

see what the man have done
                    done
see how the red blood   run
                    run

From Tokyo Rose to the Eskimos
the battleship travels
wherever he goes like Vanilla Attila
the Hun

see what the man have done
                    done

Stop lunch for the kids
then decide over brunch
how many old folks should die
by the gun

see what the man have done
                    done

If you get sick you better get better
real quick
or the illness will cost you
a ton

Hari Kari was worried about
whom he should marry
but then he married a nun

see what the man have done
done

Work like a jerk and your job
just becomes a statistical quirk
there's damned little work left
under the sun

see how the red blood run
run

Grandita Banana gets stuck
in Havana for reasons of
Bradstreet and Dun

see what the man have done
done

Murder and pillage through city
and village
raping a tree is not easy
but fun

see what the man have done
                              done
see how the red blood run
                              run

Poem for Etel Adnan Who Writes:

"So we shall say: Don't fool
yourselves.
Jesus is not coming.
We are alone"

—1983

1

I am alone
I am not coming not coming to Jesus not coming to
the telephone
not coming to the door not coming to my own true
love I am alone
I am not coming

2

Jesus forgot
Jesus came and then he left but then he forgot
He forgot why he came
He forgot to come back
And this is written in the water by the dolphins
flying like rice-paper submarines
Jesus forgot

3

Nobody died to save the world

4

Come

5

Let us break heads together

Richard Wright Was Wrong

Richard Wright was wrong
because Bigger Thomas was a whiteman
yes he was
the one does it to you
did it to Fatima Ghazzawi
17 year old Palestinian whose leg
the real Bigger Thomas blew into infinity
he's the one teaching his children to kill
for the Klan
he's the one shot off the arm of 15 year old
Brenda Rocha in the land of the Sandinistas
FORGET THE METAPHORS
                        Black man in white girl's bedroom
                        Black man at furnace
                        Black man sawing off the head
the real Bigger Thomas don't fool around
with literature
FORGET THE METAPHOR
the real Bigger Thomas
don't sleep
don't hide
don't sweat
the real Bigger Thomas
allocates this
appropriates that
incinerates
assassinates
he hates he hates he hates
he intervenes

never means what he says
he means what he does
he does it to you
he's a whiteman
he's the Grand Duke Dragon of the Ku Klux Klan
he rules Chicago
he over-rules New York
he turns the Atlantic into a floating latrine
he looks at the stars and dreams about wars
he's mean
he's the trickytreating face in the pumpkin
the inventor of sin
the skull with the candles of hell
flaming inside
he's race purity race pride
he's Son of Adolph Hitler in a Ferrari
roars into the tree that grew by mistake
in the way
he's the reason poor Richard Wright was wrong
all along
he's the real Bigger Thomas
the real Bigger Thomas
was a white man who does what he does
yes he was
yes he does it to you
yes he does

Easter Comes to the East Coast: 1981

Don' you worry about a thing
Mr. President and you too
Mr. Secretary of the State: Relax!
We not studying you guys:
NO NO NO NO NO!
This ain' real
Ain' nobody standing around
We not side by side
This ain' no major league rally
We not holding hands again
We not some thousand varieties of one fist!
This ain' no coalition
This ain' no spirit no muscle no body to stop the bullets
We not serious
NO NO NO NO NO!
And I ain' never heard about El Salvador;
I ain' never seen the children sliced
and slaughtered at the Sumpul Riverside
And I ain' never heard about Atlanta;
I ain' never seen the children strangled in the woods
And I ain' never seen marines state troopers or the police
out here killing people
And I ain' never heard about no rage no tears
no developing
rebellion
I ain' never felt no love enough to fight what's hateful
to my love

NO NO NO NO NO!
This is just a fantasy.
We just kidding around.

You watch!

Song of the Law Abiding Citizen

so hot so hot so hot so what
so hot so what so hot so hot

They made a mistake
I got more than I usually take
I got food stamps food stamps I got
so many stamps in the mail
I thought maybe I should put them on sale
How lucky I am
I got food stamps: Hot damn!
I made up my mind
to be decent and kind
to let my upright character shine
I sent 10,000 food stamps
back to the President (and his beautiful wife)
and I can't pay the rent
but I sent 10,000 food stamps
back to the President (and his beautiful wife)
how lucky I am
hot damn
They made a mistake
for Chrissake
And I gave it away to the President
I thought that was legal I thought that was kind
and I can't pay the rent
but I sent 10,000 food stamps
back back back to the President

so hot so hot so hot so what
so hot so what so hot so hot

Trucks cruisin' down the avenue
carrying nuclear garbage right next to you
and it's legal
it's radioaction ridin' like a regal
load of jewels
past the bars the cruel
school house and the church and if
the trucks wipeout or crash
or even lurch too hard around a corner
we will just be goners
and it's legal
it's radioaction ridin' regal
through the skittery city street
and don't be jittery
because it's legal
radioaction ridin' the road

Avenue A Avenue B Avenue C Avenue D
Avenue of the Americas

so hot so hot so hot so what
so hot so what so hot so hot
so hot so hot so hot so what

The way she played the piano
    the one listening was the one taken
    the one taken was the one
          into the water/
          watching the foam
          find the beautiful boulders
          dark
          easily liquid
          and true as the stone
          of that meeting/molecular
          elements of lust
          distilled by the developing
          sound
          sorrow
          sound
          fused by the need of the fingers
          to note down
          to touch upon
          to span
          to isolate
          to pound
          to syncopate
          to sound
          sorrow
          sound
          among the waters
          gathering
          corpuscular/exquisite

constellations tuning among waves
the soul itself
pitched atonal but below
the constellations tuning among waves
the soul itself

a muscular/exquisite

matter of tactful
            exact
            uproarious
heart
collecting the easily dark
liquid
look
of the beautiful boulders

in that gathering
    that water

                    for a.b.t.

look at the blackbird fall
down
into the lake
split by white speedboats full of white people
loading the atmosphere with gasoline
and noise
now
you can't drink the water
of the lake
you must drive somewhere else to buy
bottles of water to drink
beside the lake that is ten miles
long
(what I need is a change of season
a snowmobile
or a springtime tomb
that takes me from birth to 55
in six seconds)
what I need is to adjust
to the tree
without the blackbird that fell
down
into the lake

March Song

Snow knuckles melted to pearls
of black water
Face like a landslide of stars
in the dark

Icicles plunging to waken the grave
Tree berries purple and bitten
by birds

Curves of horizon squeeze
on the sky
Telephone wires glide
down the moon

Outlines of space later
pieces of land
with names like Beirut
where the game is to tear
up the whole Hemisphere
into pieces of children
and patches of sand

Asleep on a pillow the two
of us whisper we know
about apples and hot bread
and honey

Hunting for safety
and eager for peace
We follow the leaders who chew up
the land
with names like Beirut
where the game is to tear
up the whole Hemisphere
into pieces of children
and patches of sand

I'm standing in place
I'm holding your hand
and pieces of children
on patches of sand

We got crispy chicken
we got frisky chicken
we got digital chicken
we got Chicken Evergreen

We got chicken salad
we got chicken with rice
we got radar chicken
we got chicken in the first degree

but we ain't got no fried chicken.

We got Chicken Red Light
we got drive-in chicken
we got felony chicken
we got chicken gravy

but we ain't got no fried chicken.

We got half a chicken
we got 2 chickens
we got Chicken Tylenol
we got chicken on ice

but we ain't got no fried chicken.

We got King Chicken
we got chicken a la mode
we got no-lead chicken

We got chainsaw chicken
we got chicken in a chair
we got borderline chicken
we got Chicken for the Young at Heart

We got aeresol chicken
we got Chicken Guitar

but we ain't got no fried chicken.

We got Coast Guard Chicken
we got sixpack chicken
we got Chicken Las Vegas
we got chicken to burn

but we ain't got no fried chicken.

We got 10-speed chicken
we got atomic chicken
we got chicken on tape

We got day-care chicken
we got Chicken Mascara
we got second-hand chicken

but we ain't got no fried chicken.

We got dead chicken
we got chicken on the hoof
we got open admissions chicken
we got Chicken Motel

We got astronaut chicken
we got chicken to go

We got gospel chicken
we got four-wheel drive chicken
we got chain gang chicken
we got chicken transfusions

but we ain't got no fried chicken

We got wrong turn chicken
we got rough draft chicken
we got chicken sodas
we got Chicken Deluxe

but we ain't
got
no

fried chicken.

Copyright © 1983:
        June Jordan & Sara Miles

Addenda to the Papal Bull

dedicated to the Poet Nicanor Parra

The Pope thinks.
The Pope thinks all of the time.
The Pope thinks it is the duty of His
Holiness to think out loud.
The Pope thinks out loud.
The Pope thinks it is the duty of His
Holiness to publish His thoughts.
The Pope publishes His thoughts.
The Pope is thinking about peace.
He is in favor of peace.
The Pope is thinking about meat.
He is in favor of fish.
The Pope is thinking about women.
He thinks women can be acceptable.
These are the thoughts of the Pope on sex:
The Pope thinks that no sex is better than good.
The Pope thinks that good sex is better than sin.
The Pope thinks that sin happens
when sex happens when two people
want to have sex with each other.
The Pope thinks that is an example of lust.
The Pope thinks that lust is for the birds.
Marriage without sex without lust is permissible.
Remarriage is permissible only
without lackluster and lusty sex, both.
The Pope thinks that these thoughts
on peace and women and meat and sex
deserve our most obedient attention.
The Pope is thinking and thinking and thinking.
Who can deny the usefulness of His concern?

Poem for the Poet Sara Miles

Not quite enough starlight lets me write
this poem tonight without clicking the lamp
on the way the 42nd street billboard streams
electrode rumors right around the triangular
building based on that island where the U.S.
Armed Forces Recruiting Station
closed because it's raining
grants no shelter to the few pedestrians
while the big
bus boats by and taxis cruise through and cars
halt because the poet stands there
mid-river
moving words times square times words
because the cold rain
holds her thin to an ineradicable pinpoint
between traffic and inertia
searching out a Sunday flick they call The House
of All Evil while the guy who wears
the button with the one word SEX gawks
openmindedly to see the impact of minutiae
the music of such poetry that sways the racket
into sweet commotion
moving words times square times words
that pray this city
will not allow its living noise
to quiet now

for keeps

Poem for Guatemala

dedicated to Rigoberto Manchú

(With thanks to Journey to the Depths, *the testimony
of Rigoberto Manchú, translated into English
by Patricia Goedicke, October, 1982)*

No matter how loudly I call you the sound of your name
makes,the day soft
Nothing about it sticks to my throat
Guatemala
syllables that lilt into twilight and lust
Guatemala
syllables to melt bullets

They call you Indian
They called me West Indian
You learned to speak Spanish when I did
We were thirteen
I wore shoes
I ate rice and peas
The beans and the rice in your pot
brought the soldiers
to hack off your arms

"Walk like that into the kitchen!
Walk like that into the clearing!
Girl with no arms!"

81

I had been playing the piano

Because of the beans and the rice in your pot
the soldiers arrived with an axe
to claim you guerilla
girl with no arms

An Indian is not supposed to own a pot of food
An Indian is too crude
An Indian covers herself with dirt so the cold
times will not hurt her

Cover yourself with no arms!

They buried my mother in New Jersey.
Black cars carried her there.
She wore flowers and a long dress.

Soldiers pushed into your mother
and tore out her tongue
and whipped her under a tree
and planted a fly in the bleeding
places so that worms
spread through the flesh
then the dogs
then the buzzards
then the soldiers laughing
at the family of the girl
with no arms
guerilla girl
with no arms

You go with no arms
among the jungle treacheries
You go with no arms
into the mountains hunting
revenge

I watch you
walk like that
into the kitchen
walk like that
into the clearing
girl with no arms

I am learning new syllables
of revolution

Guatemala
Guatemala
Girl with no arms

On the Real World: Meditation #1. /

5 shirts
2 blouses
3 pairs of jeans and the iron's on hot
for cotton:
I press the steam trigger to begin
with the section underneath the collar
from the inside out.
Then the sleeves. Starting with the cuffs.
Now the collar wrong way before it's right.
I'm not doing so good.
Around where the sleeve joins the shoulder looks
funny.
My hand stops startled.
New like a baby there's a howling on the rise.
I switch the shirt so that the iron reaches
the front panel easily.
That howling like a long walk by the Red
Brigades for twenty years between improbable
Chinese ravines with watercolor trees
poked into a spot as graceful as clouds
missing deliberate from a revolutionary landscape printed in Japan
ebbs then returns a louder howling cold
as the long walk towards the watery
limits of the whole earth blasted by the air
become tumescent in a lonely place
inhabited by the deaf or the invisible
but querulously looming victims of such speed
in spoken pain the louder howling large

as the original canvas containing that landscape
printed in Japan almost overloaded as the howling loses
even its small voice while I
bite my lips and lower my head
hard into the ferocity of that sound
dwarfing me into someone almost immaterial
as now I smell fire
and look down all the way to the shirt
pocket
skyblue and slightly burned

the snow
nearly as soft
as the sleeping nipple
of your left breast

Who Would Be Free,
'hemselves Must Strike the Blow
—Frederick Douglass

The cow could not stand up. The deadly river
washed the feet of children. Where the cows
grazed the ground concealed invisible
charged particles that did not glow or make
a tiny sound.

It was pretty quiet.

The cow could not stand up. The deadly clouds
bemused the lovers lying on the deadly ground
to watch the widening nuclear light
commingle with the wind their bodies set
to motion.

It was pretty quiet.

The cow could not stand up.
The milk should not be sold.
The baby would not be born right.
The mother could not do anything about the baby
or the cow.

It was pretty quiet.

A Runaway Lil Bit Poem

Sometimes DeLiza get so crazy she omit
the bebop from the concrete she intimidate
the music she excruciate the whiskey she
obliterate the blow she sneeze
hypothetical at sex

Sometimes DeLiza get so crazy she abstruse
about a bar-be-cue ribs wonder-white-bread
sandwich in the car with hot sauce
make the eyes roll right to where you are
fastidious among the fried-up chicken wings

Sometimes DeLiza get so crazy she exasperate
on do they hook it up they being Ingrid
Bergman and some paranoid schizophrenic Mister
Gregory Peck-peck: Do
they hook it up?

Sometimes DeLiza get so crazy she drive
right across the water flying champagne bottles
from the bridge she last drink to close the bars she
holler kissey lips she laugh she let
you walk yourself away:

Sometimes DeLiza get so crazy!

eLiza Spend the Day in the City

DeLiza drive the car to fetch Alexis
running from she building past the pickets
make she gap tooth laugh why don't
they think up something new they picket now
for three months soon it be too cold
to care

Opposite the Thrift Shop
Alexis ask to stop at the Botanica
St. Jacques Majeur find oil to heal she
sister lying in the hospital from lymphoma
and much western drug agenda

DeLiza stop. Alexis running back
with oil and myrrh and frankincense and coal
to burn these odors free the myrrh like rocks
a baby break to pieces fit inside the palm
of long or short lifelines

DeLiza driving and Alexis
point out Nyabinghi's African emporium
of gems and cloth and Kwanza cards and clay:
DeLiza look.

Alexis opening the envelope to give DeLiza
faint gray copies of she article on refugees
from Haiti and some other thing on one white
male one
David Mayer
sixty-six
a second world war veteran
who want America to stop atomic arms
who want America to live without the nuclear death
who want it bad enough to say he'll blow
the Washington
D.C. Monument into the southside of the White House
where the First White Lady counting up she
$209,000. dollar china plates and cups and bowls
but cops blow him away
blow him/he David Mayer
man of peace
away
Alexis saying, "Shit.
He could be Jesus. Died to save you,
didn't he?"
DeLiza nod she head.
God do not seem entirely to be dead.

DeLiza Questioning Perplexities:

If Dustin Hoffaman prove
a father be a better mother than a mother

If Dustin Hoffaman prove
a man be a better woman than a woman

When do she get to see
a Betterman than Hoffaman?

November

Given those leaves why should I complain
That is not Macchu Picchu to my left
Under my feet the trees deposit lives at last
in color not dividing into class or coronation
of any kind

The slave lives in my mouth
White gates to the dark throat of my name
at fifty miles an hour I visualize a profile
leading to another language I am cowardly
to understand

A woman my age lying down at the top
of the outdoor stairs delivers her vote
her face to the stone of voice and makes
the awkward leadership swerve resolute around
her fallen body

In my room the boy stammering they
promised me a job they promised me they
do not hear the edge to the stutter
the gun under stultimultistultifying
failures of the scream

I prophesy the same unto the same
an imagery to overflow the frame
beyond the tombstone straight ahead
beyond the monologue of living normal
with the dead

Verse After Listening to Bartók play Bartók A Second Time
Or: Different Ways of Tingling All Over

now

and then

unexpectedly
unexpectedly
unexpectedly

                                                      (praying)

then

and now

oem Towards a Final Solution

In a press conference this afternoon the Secretary
of Space Development confirmed earlier reports
of a comprehensive plan nearing completion
in his Office.

Scheduled to meet with the President later
this week, Mr. Samuel B. Fierce the Third
jokingly termed the forthcoming package of proposals
"A Doozie".

The following represents a news team summary
of his remarks:

His Office will issue findings of a joint survey
of all National Parks conducted in cooperation with
the Department of the Interior in an effort to delimit
unnecessary vegetation.

His Office will recommend installation of nuclear
reactors inside low-growth residential areas of American
cities in order to encourage voluntary citizen re-
location at estimated savings to the Federal Government
of more than 2 billion dollars, yearly.

At the same time, Mr. Fierce suggested that he will recommend
quick phasing out of Federal programs for
land reclamation
described by the Secretary at one particularly light-hearted
moment during the press conference as
"Neanderthal nostalgia
for the little flowers that grow."

In addition, the Secretary indicated he will call
for the computation of food stamps as income so that,
for example, a legitimate Welfare recipient in Mississippi
will have exactly $8. a month as disposable cash.

Finally, Mr. Fierce alluded to a companion proposal
that will raise the rent for subsidized housing by 20%.

These various initiatives can be trusted to contribute
significantly to the President's economic goals and to
the development of more space, coast to coast. They
will furthermore establish the Office of
Space Development
as an increasingly powerful factor in budget-conscious
policymaking.

An unidentified reporter then queried the Secretary as to
whether this plan could fairly be translated as take
down the trees, tear-up the earth, evacuate the urban poor,
and let the people hang, generally speaking.

Mr. Fierce dismissed the question as a clear-cut attempt
at misleading and alarmist language deliberately obtuse
to the main objective of economic recovery for the nation.

Pending official release of his recommendations to
the President, the Secretary refused to comment on
the snow
falling on the stones of the cities everywhere.

1981: On Call

And even as you light
the cigarette or turn the page
blood flows from the throat of the scream

Every standing tree is quiet at night
and mute to the flood
but part of the dream

Silence will nothing redeem
into body or bud
for the actual fight

for Kimako

Kimako Baraka
1936–1984

She loved garlic
sometimes I thought she was altogether garlic
cloves small as they are thinskinned stones

She loved silk
sometimes I thought the sinews of her body
intimated silk at the atomic level of a hand

She loved poetry
sometimes I thought that she would take the words
and eat them carefully as filaments of saffron

She loved commotion
sometimes I thought a movement created Kimako
but sometimes (I thought) she created a movement

ssailant: **Antonio Moore**

1984–?

You were hungry and she
let you into her life

You grabbed her by the throat
you stabbed her in the throat
you stabbed her in the chest
you stabbed her in the back
you beat her eyes out
you beat her ears off
you smashed her skull
you busted her nose
you tore away her clothes
you tore apart her mouth

you said thank you
the only way you knew how

And I only wish for you
exactly what you deserve
for that
exactly what you deserve

It should not be the death
                not that we should gather now
                remembering that laugh between her teeth
                                that spine behind the curtain
                                that Egypt prize of window eyes

                not that we should tremble now
                remembering that we forgot
the glory gone
the old shoes on the street
the hand out for the handout

                not that we should rally now
                remembering the glitter of the tricks she lit
                                the horns
                                the drums
                                the stage

It should be the dance
It should be the dance she danced
with death

A Reagan Era Poem in Memory of Scarlet O'Hara

who said, in Gone With the Wind, *something like this:*

"As God is my witness, so help me God:
I'm going to live through this
And when it's over
If I have to lie, steal, cheat, or kill,
I'll never go hungry again."

The poem says:
"Amen!"

Apologies to All the People in Lebanon

*Dedicated to the 600,000 Palestinian men,
women, and children
who lived in Lebanon from 1948–1983.*

I didn't know and nobody told me and what
could I do or say, anyway?

They said you shot the London Ambassador
and when that wasn't true
they said so
what
They said you shelled their northern villages
and when U.N. forces reported that was not true
because your side of the cease-fire was holding
since more than a year before
they said so
what
They said they wanted simply to carve
a 25 mile buffer zone and then
they ravaged your
water supplies your electricity your
hospitals your schools your highways and byways all
the way north to Beirut because they said this
was their quest for peace
They blew up your homes and demolished the grocery
stores and blocked the Red Cross and took away doctors
to jail and they cluster-bombed girls and boys
whose bodies
swelled purple and black into twice the original size
and tore the buttocks from a four month old baby
and then

they said this was brilliant
military accomplishment and this was done
they said in the name of self-defense they said
that is the noblest concept
of mankind isn't that obvious?
They said something about never again and then
they made close to one million human beings homeless
in less than three weeks and they killed or maimed
40,000 of your men and your women and your children

But I didnt know and nobody told me and what
could I do or say, anyway?

They said they were victims. They said you were
Arabs.
They called   your apartments and gardens   guerilla
strongholds.
They called   the screaming devastation
that they created   the rubble.
Then they told you to leave, didn't they?

Didn't you read the leaflets that they dropped
from their hotshot fighter jets?
They told you to go.
One hundred and thirty-five thousand
Palestinians in Beirut and why
didn't you take the hint?
Go!
There was the Mediterranean: You
could walk into the water and stay
there.
What was the problem?

I didn't know and nobody told me and what
could I do or say, anyway?

Yes, I did know it was the money I earned as a poet that
paid
for the bombs and the planes and the tanks
that they used to massacre your family

But I am not an evil person
The people of my country aren't so bad

You can't expect but so much
from those of us who have to pay taxes and watch
American tv

You see my point;

I'm sorry.
I really am sorry.

Thunder.
More thunder.
Lightning.
Thunder.
More thunder.
More thunder.
The rain reaches me through the window
nine feet away.
I read your letter again.
Lightning.
More thunder.
More. More. More thunder.
I turn out the lights.
The curtains swing to the left.
Rain becomes the coloring of the air.
Hailstones attack the roof of my room.
Like marbles.
More. More. More thunder.
I am afraid to close the window.
The blue spruce cracks.
And crashes among the marbles.
Its trunk slashed to the flesh
jaggedly.
I feel like a woman
who says to herself:

"That kid is leaning too far
out of the car.
My God.
The kid has fallen out.
On his head."

Then wonders where
should she make her report.

nother Poem About the Man

the man who brought you the garbage can
                        the graveyard
                        the grossout
                        the grimgram
                        the grubby grabbing
                        bloody blabbing nightly news
                        now brings you
                        Grenada

helicopters grating nutmeg trees
rifles shiny on the shellshocked sand
the beautiful laundry of the bombs falling into fresh air
artillery and tanks up against a halfnaked girl
and her boyfriend

another great success
brought to you
by trash delivering more trash to smash
and despoil the papaya
the breadfruit and bloodroot
shattered and bloodspattered
from freedom
rammed down the throat
of Grenada now Grenada she
no sing no more

Grenada now Grenada she
no sing no more she lose
she sky
to yankee invaders
Grenada now Grenada she
no sing no more

Into the gnat infested twilight of the woods
we walked across pine needles stuck
in the soon to be moonlit mud
discussing the cities of the world
as far away as Rome

Hovering like the suspicion of a freshwater
pond in the forest or what water implies
to a wilderness grown by one tree at a time
was the music interrupted by the piano tuner
earlier that day

Almost home again we saw the piano tuner
in his pickup truck. With his wife and child
beside him he keyed the ignition.
The engine burst into flames.
Flames flew to his face.
He went to a telephone for help.
While waiting around he played
Chopin's Revolutionary Etude
on the well-tuned piano
rather well.

Outside
his wife and child
watching the truck burn.

War Verse

Something there is that sure must love a plane
No matter how many you kill with what kind of
bombs or how much blood you manage to spill
you never will hear the cries of pain

Something there is that sure must love a plane
The pilots are never crazy or mean
and bombing a hospital's quick and it's clean
and how could you call such precision insane?

Something there is that sure must love a plane!

oem Written To The Heavy Rain
Through the Trees
r An Update on The Moonlight Sonata

Where are you?
Torso precise at the corner of the wall.
Eye casting me into a mystery.
Hand of the hungry and wrong.

They drink.
They dance.
They shoot.

We drink.
We dance.
We don't.

Where are you?
Quietly.
Quick.
Keen.
Close.

I sleep parallel to the river.
I move without shadow.
I stand below the catclysms of the moon.

By myself.

Am No More and I Am No Less

As the Lebanese disqualify the Lebanese
As the Lebanese soldier scalps the head
    of the Lebanese civilian
As the Lebanese man rebukes the Lebanese
    woman
As the Lebanese girl pretends she is not
    Lebanese
I wonder when they will organize the rest
    of us
to evict the children from the hospital ward
to bulldoze the babies crawling among the rocks
to declare even the last refuge from our
    self-hatred

illegal.

1980: Note to the League of Women Voters

Dear Ladies:

As a child my parents taught me not
to deal with bullies, fools or bums.
Strangers were forbidden. Kooks excluded.
Perverts ostracized. In addition every grown man
was my enemy unless (in some constructive way)
he proved himself a member of my family.

Now I am a woman of modest abilities: I
cannot well discriminate between disgusting
and obscene between incompetent
and criminal between apocalyptic
and malodorous between blind
and deaf between
ruthless and blundering between inertia
and insanity between one lie and another
lie

For these reasons I am forced to decline
your invitation to the vote: I am moreover forced
to decline your remarkable attributions
of responsibility as when you say
it's up to me:

What's up to me?

On Life After Life

r the Poet, Nancy Morejón

If you take three or four tulips from a cold
day
lavender tulips for example
and place them solid as a hot
room
where people do not touch
even the walls
they will forgive the shrivelling
of their petals finally
but they will not forget the heat
of the hand
that carried them blooming
into the palm of your dream

Adrienne's Poem: On The Dialectics of The Diatonic Scale

Supposing everytime I hit this key
somebody
crumples to the ground or stops
breathing for a minute or begins to strangle
in the crib

Supposing everytime I play this chord
ribs
smash
brain-cells shrink
and a woman loses all of her hair

Supposing everytime I follow a melody
the overtones irradiate five Phillipino
workers
burning their bodies
to bone

A-Flat. *A*. *A*-Sharp.
C. F. G. C.
Suppose my music is a hyper-
homicidal harp
and I'm just playing

To end my pestering my friend
said okay I'll come over and show you how you dred
your hair. She came by and told me I
should take a shower and apply a little bit
of plain shampoo then rinse.
I did and when I asked her, "Well, now what!"
She said, "That's it!"
And I been dredding ever since.

Poor Form

That whole way to Delphi
The children wrecked loaves of bread
smeared cheese banged each other
on the nose
and I must admit
I tried to obliterate such dread
disturbance of the dead the bother
of the beeline to the rose
the yowling of the healthy

Hoping to hear the gods
Having to wait on goats
we drove
not very fast
against the freeze that height promotes
the odds
against the living
that don't last

In bed
your hair beside my face
I do not sing
instead
I brace against the ending

What kind of a person would kill Black children?
What kind of a person could persuade eighteen
different Black children to get into a car or
a truck or a van?
What kind of a person could kill or kidnap
these particular
Black children:

> Edward Hope Smith, 14 years old, dead
> Alfred James Evans, 14 years old, dead
> Yosef Bell, 9 years old, dead
> Milton Harvey, 14 years old, dead
> Angel Lanier, 12 years old, dead
> Eric Middlebrooks, 14 years old, dead
> Christopher Richardson, 11 years old, dead
> Aaron Wyche, 11 years old, dead
> LaTanya Wilson, 7 years old, dead
> Anthony B. Carter, 9 years old, dead
> Earl Lee Terrell, 10 years old, dead
> Clifford Jones, 13 years old, dead
> Aaron Jackson, Jr., 9 years old, dead
> Patrick Rogers, 16 years old, dead
> Charles Stevens, 12 years old, dead
> Jeffrey Lamar Mathis, 10 years old, missing
> Darron Glass, 10 years old, missing
> Lubie "Chuck" Geter, 14 years old, dead

What kind of a person could kill a Black child
and then kill another Black child and then
kill another Black child and then kill another
Black child and then kill another
Black child and then kill another Black
child
and stay above suspicion?
What about the police?
What about somebody Black?
What sixteen year old would say no to a cop?
What seven year old would say no thanks to me?
What is an overreaction to murder?
What kind of a person could kill a Black
child and then kill a Black child and then
kill a Black child?

What kind of a person are you?
What kind of a person am I?

What makes you so sure?

What kind of a person could save a Black child?

What kind of a people will lay down its
life for the lives of our children?

What kind of a people are we?

Notes Towards Home

My born on 99th Street Uncle when he went to Canada
used to wash and polish the car long before coffee
every morning outside his room in the motel
"Because," he said, "That way they thought I lived
around there; you ever hear of a perfectly clean car
travelling all the way from Brooklyn to Quebec?"

My mother left the barefoot roads of St. Mary's
in Jamaica for the States where she wore
stockings even in a heat wave and repeatedly
advised me never to wear tacky underwear
"That way," she said, "if you have an accident
when they take you to a hospital they'll know you
come from a home."

After singing God Bless America Kate Smith
bellowed the willies out of Bless This House O
Lord We Pray/Make It Safe By Night and Day
but my cousin meant Lord keep June
and her Boris Karloff imitations out of the hall
and my mother meant Lord keep my husband out
of my way and I remember I used to mean Lord
just pretty please get me out of here!

But everybody needs a home
so at least you have someplace to leave
which is where most other folks will say
you must be coming from

Relativity

It's 5 after 4 a.m. and nothing but my own
motion stirs throughout the waiting air
the rain completely purged earlier and all
day long. I could call
you now but that would join you to this
restless lying down and getting up to list
still another act I must commit
tomorrow if I ever sleep if I ever stop
sleeping long enough to act upon the space
between this comatose commotion
and the next time I can look into your
face. I hope you're laughing at the cans
of soup the house to clean the kitchen curtains
I will wash and iron
like so many other promises I make
myself: to sweep the stairs down
to the front door
and to answer every letter down to no
thanks.
    My own motion
does not satisfy tonight and later
in the daylight I'll be speeding through the streets
a secret messenger a wakeup agent walking
backwards maybe walking sideways
but for damn sure headed possibly southeast
as well as every other whichway
in your absolute
direction

Roots for A.B.T.

There is something wonderful about the limits of a tree
But not most wonderful:

There is the flag
There is the licenseplate
Where are the trees?

Silently astir under the nervous covering of one
finger
of your hands
the veins invisible to that skin that will
not conceal the joining of the parts
the sequence
the comprehensive present tense
allowing for all alchemies
of your determination

They grow there
inside the possible and everlasting
grasp
of your own breath
your own
changeable air

Home: January 29, 1984

I can tell
because the ashtray was cleaned out
because the downstairs coconut is still full of milk
because actually nothing was left
except two shells hinged together pretty tough
at the joint
I can tell
because the in-house music now includes
the lying down look of gold and your shoulders
because there is no more noise in my head
because one room two hallways two flights of stairs
and the rest of northamerica remain
to be seen in this movie about why
I am trying to write this poem

                              not a letter
                              not a proclamation
                              not a history

I am trying to write this poem
because I can tell
because it's way after midnight and so what
I can tell
eyes open or shut
I can tell
George Washington did not sleep
here
I can tell
it was you
I can tell
it really was
you

he Cedar Trees of Lebanon

Bursting soft but kept by the structure of a spine
the green parts of the tree cloud under the clouds.
Under the axe the branches bleed red
dust. The tree bleeds red. The blood
of the cedar is red blood red body
enfolded by unmistakable brown skin.

At the end of this century massacre
remains invisible unless the victim's
skin reads white.

Night air and the smoke from the chimney
puffs into a humid atmosphere obsessed
by particles from burned up cedar trees
a smell so defiantly sweet
the stars freeze to resist that violent and swollen
odor of a life transformed by fire.

At the end of this century massacre
becomes a cluster of phosphorus
events described by a woman carrying
a mattress on her head without
a destination.

At the end of this century a girl
stands her ground next to a tree
the Cedrus Libani
that the thunder does not shake
that the lightning cannot strike down

"I know it's an unfortunate way to say it, but
do you think you can put this massacre
on the back burner now?"

The Beirut Jokebook

1. June 8, 1982:   This is not an invasion.

2. July 9, 1982:   This is a ceasefire.

3. July 15, 1982:   This is a ceasefire.

4. July 30, 1982:   This ceasefire is strained.

5. August 4, 1982:   This is not an invasion.

6. As a gesture of humanity we ask you to please pile all of your clothes and food and pots and pans and furniture and children on a bicycle and leave your homes. Our planes will be along, shortly.

7. You could go to the Sudan.

8. As another humanitarian gesture we have turned off the water and the electricity in order to speed peaceful negotiations.

9. What has 500,000 people and flies?

The words sliding from the large glass table
into the still river
tiger lilies diluted by the windows of a gray sky
On the 36th floor of a Manhattan apartment building I try
to understand French
for the sake of Adrian Diop who thought
he would teach me by speaking so fast
I lost my own name among the messages from Senegal
for the sake of Etel Adnan who thought I would know
because she slipped her words under the feet of
Lebanese children
for the sake of the workmen who smash the cathedral
that does not rise into bread
for the sake of a city where no river stays
still
the same river.

Moving Towards Home

"Where is Abu Fadi," she wailed.
"Who will bring me my loved one?"
New York Times 9/20/82

I do not wish to speak about the bulldozer and the
red dirt
not quite covering all of the arms and legs
Nor do I wish to speak about the nightlong screams
that reached
the observation posts where soldiers lounged about
Nor do I wish to speak about the woman who shoved
her baby
into the stranger's hands before she was led away
Nor do I wish to speak about the father whose sons
were shot
through the head while they slit his own throat before
the eyes
of his wife
Nor do I wish to speak about the army that lit continuous
flares into the darkness so that the others could see
the backs of their victims lined against the wall
Nor do I wish to speak about the piled up bodies and
the stench
that will not float
Nor do I wish to speak about the nurse again and
again raped
before they murdered her on the hospital floor
Nor do I wish to speak about the rattling bullets that
did not
halt on that keening trajectory

Nor do I wish to speak about the pounding on the
doors and
the breaking of windows and the hauling of families into
the world of the dead
I do not wish to speak about the bulldozer and the
red dirt
not quite covering all of the arms and legs
because I do not wish to speak about unspeakable events
that must follow from those who dare
"to purify" a people
those who dare
"to exterminate" a people
those who dare
to describe human beings as "beasts with two legs"
those who dare
"to mop up"
"to tighten the noose"
"to step up the military pressure"
"to ring around" civilian streets with tanks
those who dare
to close the universities
to abolish the press
to kill the elected representatives
of the people who refuse to be purified
those are the ones from whom we must redeem
the words of our beginning

because I need to speak about home
I need to speak about living room
where the land is not bullied and beaten into
a tombstone
I need to speak about living room
where the talk will take place in my language
I need to speak about living room
where my children will grow without horror
I need to speak about living room where the men
of my family between the ages of six and sixty-five
are not
marched into a roundup that leads to the grave
I need to talk about living room
where I can sit without grief without wailing aloud
for my loved ones
where I must not ask where is Abu Fadi
because he will be there beside me
I need to talk about living room
because I need to talk about home

I was born a Black woman
and now
I am become a Palestinian
against the relentless laughter of evil
there is less and less living room
and where are my loved ones?

It is time to make our way home.

Other titles from THUNDER'S MOUTH PRESS

About the Author

The poet **June Jordan** was born in Harlem and raised
in the Bedford-Stuyvesant neighborhood of Brooklyn.
Author of several award-winning books (the novel
His Own Where was chosen by the *New York Times*
as one of the Outstanding Books of the Year in 1971
and in 1972 was a finalist for the National Book
Award), she has to date published a total of fifteen.
Her poems, articles, essays, and reviews have
appeared in *Black World, First World, Ms., The New
York Times, The New Republic, The Nation, The Village Voice, Encore, Essence, 13th Moon, Partisan Review, Evergreen Review,* and *American Poetry Review.* Represented in numerous anthologies, she is
a member of the board of Directors for Poets and
Writers, Inc., and The Center for Constitutional
Rights.

In addition to her many political activities, she has
also worked in film and city planning and is now
writing for the theater. She has taught at City College of the City University of New York, Sarah Law-
rence College, Connecticut College, and Yale University. Currently she is Professor of English at SUNY
at Stony Brook.

In 1969 Ms. Jordan received a Rockefeller Grant in
Creative Writing. In 1970 she received the Prix de
Rome in Environmental Design. Reed Lecturer Bar-
nard College 1976. In 1978 she received a C.A.P.S.
grant in creative writing. NEA Fellowship 1982.

Living Room is the sixth volume of her poetry.

7955